☞ **P9-CEY-146**

No longer property of
Ventura County Library

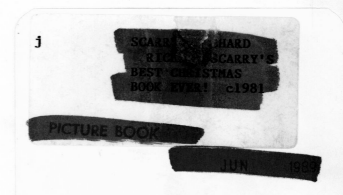

j   SCARRY, RICHARD
      RICHARD SCARRY'S
      BEST CHRISTMAS
      BOOK EVER!   c1981

      PICTURE BOOK

                    JUN   1989

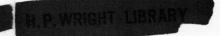

H. P. WRIGHT LIBRARY

PRM

DEMCO

Jingle Bells J. Pierpont

Richard Scarry's
Best Christmas Book Ever!

Random House  **New York**

Copyright © 1981 by Richard Scarry. All rights reserved under International
and Pan-American Copyright Conventions. Published in the United States by
Random House, Inc., New York, and simultaneously in Canada by Random
House of Canada Limited, Toronto.

Library of Congress Cataloging in Publication Data: Scarry, Richard. Richard
Scarry's Best Christmas book ever. SUMMARY: The inhabitants of Busytown
prepare for Christmas in this collection of stories, songs, and holiday
activities.   1. Christmas stories.   2. Children's stories, American.
[1. Christmas stories. 2. Christmas music. 3. Short stories.   4. Handicraft]
I. Title.   II. Title: Best Christmas book ever.   PZ7.S327Rg   1981   [E]
81-5172   ISBN: 0-394-84936-1 (trade); 0-394-94936-6 (lib. bdg.)   AACR2
Manufactured in the United States of America   5 6 7 8 9 0

Christmas Is Coming!

Busytown is getting ready for Christmas. The fire fighters are stringing lights on the buildings. The stores are crowded with shoppers. Everyone is busy. Look! There's Big Hilda, Huckle Cat, and his sister, Sally, in a big sleigh. Lowly Worm is pulling it with his appletractor. Now where are they going?

They are going to get a Christmas tree!
Farmer Pig has many beautiful pine trees
on his farm. Maybe he will give them one.
When he hears how they are going to use
the tree, Farmer Pig is happy to help.

TIMBER!

Huckle and Sally are too little to cut the
tree, but they are big enough to gather pine
branches for wreaths and decorations!

Big Hilda chops down the tree.
It is the biggest tree on the farm.
Here it comes! Timber-r-r-r!

They all help put the tree on the sleigh. "Come see the tree when we get it trimmed," says Huckle. "I'll try," says Farmer Pig, who is snowed in.

Lowly drives the sleigh back to town. They put the tree up in the town square and decorate it with lights and ornaments. Lowly puts a star at the top. Everyone comes to admire the tree—even Farmer Pig. Now Busytown is *really* ready for Christmas.

Doctor Bones Is Good All Year Round

All year round Doctor Bones is busy calling on his sick patients. Sometimes it is very hard for him to make his house calls. In the winter his car often gets stuck in the snow.

When the streets are icy, he must drive very carefully to avoid an accident. Look out, Doctor Bones! Your car is skidding on the ice!

Sometimes in the spring it rains so hard that the streets become flooded. Then his car stops dead. Surprise, Doctor Bones, that puddle is too deep to drive through!

Often he gets stuck in the mud. It is hard work—and very messy— to push the car out.

But Doctor Bones never gives up. His sick patients appreciate how hard he works for them. "We will remember you at Christmas," they all tell him.

Mrs. Cat does not complain about the bumpy ride to the hospital. She is thankful that the good Doctor Bones can take her there.

Look out for that curve, Doctor! Too late! His car goes over the guard rail and falls into the sea. But Captain Pig saves him.

MERRY CHRISTMAS

Then Christmas comes, and guess what? His patients all remember to remember him. They give him a brand-new helicopter. Now he will have no problem visiting them. Merry Christmas, Doctor Bones, the Flying Doctor!

Grouchy Mr. Gronkle

Mr. Gronkle is a grouch. He grumbles and growls at everybody. But he grumbles most of all at children. "Children? What are they good for, anyway?" he mumbles to himself. When he sees a child, he snarls, "Get out of my way, kid!"

Mr. Gronkle is very rich. He lives in a big house with a pond out front. In the winter he could skate on his frozen pond. But he doesn't. Mr. Gronkle doesn't believe in having fun.

And he doesn't believe in having friends. He lives alone in that big old house. Why, he won't even let some-one come in to help him clean his house. It looks like a pig's pen.

One fine day just before Christmas, Lowly Worm suggests that they all go ice skating on Mr. Gronkle's pond.

"We should ask his permission first," says Huckle Cat. "Oh, I'm sure Mr. Gronkle won't mind," says Lowly.

But Mr. Gronkle DOES mind! He is furious. He runs down to the frozen pond swinging his walking stick. He runs onto the ice . . .

Look out, Lowly!

OOPS!!

Mr. Gronkle slips.

CRRAACK! Right through the ice he goes and into the freezing water.

"Help! Save me!" he cries. He tries to climb out, but the ice cracks more. He can't get out by himself. At first the children feel that it serves nasty old Mr. Gronkle right. But then they begin to feel sorry for him.

"He'll soon freeze to death in that cold water," says Huckle. "We must help him."

"Don't leave me to die!" shouts Mr. Gronkle when he sees the children running off.

But they are not leaving him. They are going to find a ladder.

Huckle puts the ladder on the ice.

Lowly winds himself like a rope around Mr. Gronkle's nose. "What are those terrible children doing?" wonders Mr. Gronkle. Then they all pull on Lowly.

Slowly they pull Mr. Gronkle out of the water and onto the ice. "You're the best rope ever, Lowly," says Huckle.

"Now I know what children are good for," says Mr. Gronkle. "They're good for saving cranky, grouchy Mr. Gronkle."

Mr. Gronkle promises to change his nasty ways. He starts by having a wonderful Christmas party for all the children. He has such a good time that he decides to turn his house into a play center!

Now cranky, grouchy Mr. Gronkle is called cheerful, friendly Mr. G. He's always busy seeing that the children have a good time at his house.
Merry Christmas, Mr. Gronkle!

Postman Pig and Aunt Kitty

Postman Pig is busier than ever at Christmastime. There are so many Christmas cards and presents to deliver. Today he has a letter for old Aunt Kitty. That pleases him because Aunt Kitty lives alone and has no friends.

Aunt Kitty is pleased to get the letter, too. "Oh, do come in and have a cup of hot chocolate while I read my letter," she says.

Aunt Kitty reads the letter and bursts into tears. "Oh, boo, hoo, hoo!" she cries. "My niece won't be able to visit me on Christmas. I will be all alone." Postman Pig starts to cry, too. "Boo, hoo, hoo!"

Going back to the post office, Postman Pig meets Lowly and tells him Aunt Kitty's sad news. They both cry. "We must do something for her," says Lowly.

Then Lowly tells Huckle Cat about lonely Aunt Kitty.

And Huckle tells his mother. "Boo, hoo, hoo!" he cries.

Mother Cat tells Ma Pig. "Oh, isn't that a shame!" they say.

Ma Pig tells Sergeant Murphy. Even the brave sergeant cries! "Boo, hoo, hoo!"

 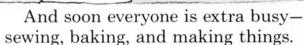

Soon everyone in Busytown hears the sad story of Aunt Kitty.

And soon everyone is extra busy— sewing, baking, and making things.

Then, on Christmas morning, who do you think comes to visit Aunt Kitty? EVERYONE in Busytown! And each with a wonderful present. Aunt Kitty is so happy to see that she has so many friends after all.

Trouble at Santa's Workshop

In Santa's workshop there are hundreds of elves who work, work, work all day long making toys for Santa to bring on Christmas.

Some of the elves want to work all night long, too. But Santa won't let them. "You need a good night's sleep to work well the next day," he tells them. And they can't disobey Santa—even if they would like to—because he locks up all the tools at night.

Then one morning Santa discovers that he has lost the key to his tool closet!

Santa and Mrs. Claus look everywhere for the key. But they can't find it.

"I know!" says Santa. "I'll call my good friend Lowly Worm and ask him to bring me some keys that might fit."

Lowly is happy to help—if he can.

Lowly goes to the locksmith's and gets big keys and little keys, thick keys and thin keys.

Then he gets into his applecopter and flies to the North Pole, where Santa and his elves are waiting for him.

Santa takes Lowly to the locked tool closet door.
"One of these keys will surely fit," says Lowly.

He tries one.
It doesn't work.

He tries another and another
and another. But none of the
keys that Lowly has will fit
the lock.

"This is terrible!" sighs Lowly.
"If I can't open this lock, there
will be no toys for Christmas." He
puts his eye right up to the keyhole
and looks inside. Then suddenly
he has an idea!

He takes off his sneaker.

Then he takes off his sock.

And he wiggles his bare foot around.

He puts his foot in the keyhole and twists and turns his toe.

Click, goes the lock! Lowly Key smiles. "I opened it!"

The elves rush to get their tools and hurry back to their workbenches. There will be toys for Christmas after all. Hurrah!

"May I make a toy too before I leave?" Lowly asks Santa. "Please do!" says Santa. "We need all we can make."

Then Santa thanks him for all his help, and Lowly hops into his applecopter and flies safely home.

Maybe one of the toys you get for Christmas will be the very one that Lowly made!

NAILS GLUE BUTTONS

Big Hilda Helps Santa

It is the night before Christmas, and Santa is on his way to bring presents to boys and girls all over the world. Here he is over Busytown. His first stop will be at Sergeant Murphy's house. Santa has some very nice toys for little Bridget Murphy.

CRASH! Santa's sleigh lands too hard and one of the runners breaks.

"What's all that noise up on my roof?" asks a sleepy Sergeant Murphy.

Sergeant Murphy climbs onto the roof. He is very surprised to see Santa with his broken sleigh.

"You're in real trouble now, Santa. I don't know how to repair your sleigh, but I will get Mr. Fixit."

Sergeant Murphy jumps on his motorcycle and hurries to Mr. Fixit's house. He pounds on the door. A sleepy Mr. Fixit comes out and off they go to fix Santa's sleigh.

But Mr. Fixit is still half asleep and clumsily breaks the other runner. Santa is furious! "Now look what you've done!" he shouts.

"What's all that noise about?" calls Big Hilda from her house. Sergeant Murphy tells her and she says, "I'll be right over!"

So Big Hilda plows through the snow, carrying her skis.

"Here, Santa," she says. "You can fix your sleigh with these skis."

Mr. Fixit offers to nail the skis to the sleigh. "No, thanks!" says Santa. "I will do it myself!" Now Santa can deliver the rest of his presents.

And what do you suppose Big Hilda finds in her stocking on Christmas morning?
A NEW PAIR OF SKIS!

The Best Christmas Present Ever

On Christmas Eve Pickles and Penny Pig
hang up their stockings by the fireplace.
It is cozy inside, but outside it is snowing
hard. "I do hope this blizzard won't keep
Santa from visiting us," says Penny.

They leave a plate of cookies and
a cup of hot chocolate for Santa.

Then off to bed they go to dream about
what Santa will bring them.

Daddy, Mommy, and Aunty Rose
stay up. Aunty Rose has come to
visit for a few days, and they have
a lot of things to talk about.

Later Daddy puts on his cap and coat and goes out to the garage.

He shovels a path through the deep snow to the street. Now why is he doing that at this time of night?

Look! Mommy is in the car with Daddy. They must be crazy to go for a ride on such a snowy night.

Oh, oh! They are stuck in a snowdrift! But a tow truck with a snowplow comes to their rescue.

In the morning Pickles and Penny rush in
to see what Santa has brought them.

Pickles got a drum, a sled, skis, a paint set, a fire
truck, and some good storybooks.

Penny got a doll, a dollhouse, a fire truck just like
her brother's, ice skates, and some books about dinosaurs.

Aunty Rose got ten bottles of
perfume and two handkerchiefs.

Daddy got a new shaving brush and ten neckties.
How will he ever decide which one to wear first!

Then Pickles and Penny ask about Mommy.
What did SHE get? And where IS she?
"Mommy had to go downtown last night to
get her present. It is a very special
Christmas present," says Daddy, who is
as happy as can be. "Get your hats and
coats and let's go see what she got."

They drive downtown and stop at the Busytown Hospital.
Guess who they see inside the hospital?

There is Mommy with a little newborn baby called
Nicholas. Now, isn't that the best Christmas present
ever for the whole family!

Mr. Frumble Helps Out

Who is that dressed like Santa?
Why, it is Mr. Frumble! He is
invited to the Cat family's house
for Christmas dinner, and he wants
to thank them in his own special way.

Huckle, Sally, and Lowly are
playing by the fireplace.
Suddenly they hear a noise.
Then some black soot falls
from the chimney. Can Santa
be coming again!

"Help! I'm stuck!" cries a voice. It is coming from
the chimney. Father Cat jumps up and rushes to the
fireplace. He reaches up the chimney and they all
help pull. Out pops a very sooty Mr. Frumble!
"Merry Christmas! Ho! Ho! Ho!" says Santa Frumble.

First he brushes the dirty soot off his suit.
It falls on the nice clean rug. Then he offers
to help with the dinner. He runs toward the
kitchen—and right into the Christmas tree!

CRASH! The tree falls over and Huckle and Lowly
have to set it back up again.

Mr. Frumble decides to bake
a cake, but he spills the batter
all over the floor.

The potatoes he is
cooking explode all
over the kitchen.

And the turkey he is roasting
burns up. Smoke pours all over
the house and fire fighters
have to be called in.

"Thank you, Mr. Frumble, but I really
don't need your help," says Mother Cat.

"I'll just mop up this water," says Mr. Frumble. He
swings the mop so hard that he breaks a table leg.
Everything crashes to the floor. Mother Cat will never
finish making the dinner with him around!

She gently pushes Mr. Frumble
toward the door. But he
trips and crashes into the
refrigerator. Now there is
another big mess on the floor!

At last Mother Cat is alone in her kitchen. She
cleans up everything and then makes a wonderful
Christmas dinner. The children carry the food to
the table. She won't let Mr. Frumble carry anything!

Mmmm! The dinner is delicious and everyone enjoys it—until butterfingers Mr. Frumble drops the gravy boat and knocks over a big pitcher of grape juice. Now Mother Cat's beautiful tablecloth is bright purple.

Now it is time for dessert. And Mr. Frumble has a very special dessert surprise for the Cat family and their guests. It is a HUGE cherry pie. He goes to the kitchen to get it.

Here he comes now. Just look at the size of that pie! It is so big that Mr. Frumble has to balance it on his head. My, it is going to taste good! He walks very slowly and very carefully. Oh, oh, watch your step, Mr. Frumble, there is a toy on the floor. Ohhh, no . . .

You guessed it!
Well, this is certainly the messiest Merry Christmas ever. But everyone seems to be having a cherry good time!

What Shall We Give Grandma for Christmas?

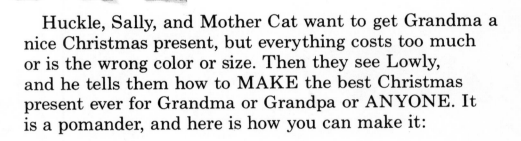

Huckle, Sally, and Mother Cat want to get Grandma a nice Christmas present, but everything costs too much or is the wrong color or size. Then they see Lowly, and he tells them how to MAKE the best Christmas present ever for Grandma or Grandpa or ANYONE. It is a pomander, and here is how you can make it:

Get a nice big apple and a jar of cloves.

Stick the cloves into the apple until it is completely covered with cloves.

Then tie a pretty red ribbon around the apple, and you have a sweet-smelling pomander. Grandma can put it in her clothes drawer or closet, and it will smell sweet and spicy for many Christmases.

A Visit to Grandma's House

On Christmas morning Father Cat opens the front door and discovers that it has snowed very hard during the night.

"I hope we can get to Grandma's house today," he says.

He shovels a path in the deep snow from the garage to the street. My, that's hard work!

They start on their way but run into a big snowdrift. Now they are STUCK!

Farmer Pig and little Bugdozer come to pull them out. But they get STUCK, too!

Mr. Fixit comes in his tow truck. Guess what? He gets stuck. Now everyone is STUCK!

Along comes Lowly with his appletractor and sleigh.

And off they go to Grandma's house, singing "Jingle Bells" all the way.

Grandma is happy to see them. Look how pleased
she is with her pomander apples! Now her clothes
will smell lovely all year long. It's such a nice
present . . . and from such nice grandchildren!

A Visit to Grandma's House Game

These are the rules for the game on the next
two pages.

You will need four pennies, and a small
square of construction paper for each player
with his or her initials on it. Have your mom or
dad cut them out and help you initial them.

1. Who goes first? Each player drops the four
pennies. The player with the most "heads" goes
first, the one with the next most goes second,
and so on. Each player starts with his or her
"piece" (the square of paper) at the Cat family's
house.

2. How to move. When it's your turn, drop the
four pennies. The number of heads you get is
the number of spaces you should move your
piece along the road to Grandma's house. If you
land on a space with another player's piece on it
already, you lose your next turn.

3. Rewards and penalties. When you land on
a reward or penalty space, do what it says.

4. Who wins? The first player to reach
Grandma's house wins the game.
He or she gets a kiss from Grandma.

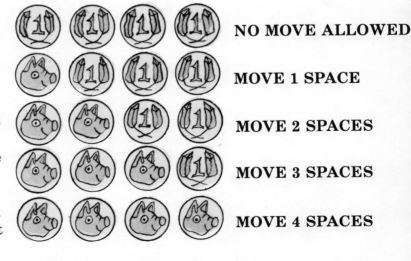

NO MOVE ALLOWED

MOVE 1 SPACE

MOVE 2 SPACES

MOVE 3 SPACES

MOVE 4 SPACES

Off the road. Go back 2.

Red light. Lose 1 turn.

Step on gas. Go ahead 2.

Person crossing road. Lose 1 turn.

Go down hill. Go ahead 2.

Through the woods. Go ahead 2.

Blizzard. Lose 1 turn.

Off the road. Go back 1.

Engine stalls. Go back 1.

Windshield frosted. Lose 1 turn.

Hen in road. Go back 1.

Grandma's House
FINISH
and wipe the snow off your feet!

Sing "Jingle Bells." Go ahead 3.

Smile. Go ahead 1.

Flat tire. Lose 1 turn.

The Bad Twins

Once there were twins named Abe and Babe who were so bad that everyone called them "double trouble." They were really horrid!

They liked to argue and fight and push people in the mud.

They always shouted and rudely interrupted other people.

They thought it was fun to break things that didn't belong to them.

At the playground they took toys away from little children.

They ate with their fingers and made a mess of everything. Their table manners were terrible! Even their mother had to agree that if there was anything bad, rude, or nasty that could be done, they would do it.

Santa does not bring nice presents to bad boys and girls. Instead, he fills their stockings with dirty lumps of coal.

So on Christmas morning Abe and Babe got a big surprise. Two HUGE sacks of coal were all that Santa brought them. That's how bad they were!

Abe and Babe were very sad. They knew that Santa was punishing them for being so bad. "We must learn to be good," they said to each other.

Outside everyone was playing with their new sleds. Abe and Babe sadly watched them.

"I wish we had a sled," said Abe.

"And I wish we had some electricity," said Sergeant Murphy. "The snowstorm broke the electrical lines, and without electricity there are going to be a lot of cold houses and uncooked Christmas dinners."

Abe and Babe felt sorry for all the people whose Christmas day would be spoiled. "This is our chance to be good," Abe said to Babe. They told Sergeant Murphy their plan. "That's a splendid idea!" he said.

Sergeant Murphy called the children together and told them to take their sleds to the twins' house.

"Not on your life!" said the children. "Those twins are double trouble." But Sergeant Murphy assured them that everything would be all right.

When the children got to the twins' house, Abe and Babe dragged their big sacks of coal outside. Then they filled a paper bag with coal for each child.

The children gave the coal to their families to burn in picnic grills. That Christmas all the dinners in Busytown were cooked on picnic grills!

The dinners were delicious! And the grills gave off enough heat to keep the houses warm until the electricity came back on.

Santa always leaves a few extra toys at the firehouse to give to children he might have missed. So when Santa heard about Abe and Babe's good deed, he called the fire chief right away and told him to see that Abe and Babe got some really nice Christmas presents.

From that day on, the bad twins became good twins. And every Christmas after that, the twins received a tiny piece of coal in their stockings to remind them of their good deed on that cold Christmas day.

Christmas Words

chimney

star

wreath

candle

ornaments

cards

dining room table

tree

stockings

fireplace

Christmas presents

pie

cook

kitchen

cookies

turkey

snowball

carolers

snowman

church

snow

bell

Daddy's new necktie

mistletoe

saucer sled

sled

skis

snowfort

sack

ice

hockey stick

skates

Mr. Frumble Santa Claus

skating rink

footprints in the snow

Silent Night

Joseph Mohr

Franz Gruber

2.
Silent night, holy night!
Shepherds quake at the sight;
Glories stream from heaven afar,
Heavenly hosts sing *Alleluia,*
Christ the Savior is born!
Christ the Savior is born!

3.
Silent night, holy night!
Son of God, love's pure light
Radiant beams from Thy holy face,
With the dawn of redeeming grace,
Jesus, Lord, at Thy Birth,
Jesus, Lord, at Thy Birth.